Back to Normal

Back to Normal

Adapted by Jane Mason and Sara Hines Stephens

Based on "Back to PCA" written by Dan Schneider
"Time Capsule" written by Steve Holland

Based on the television series *Zoey 101* created by Dan Schneider

Scholastic Canada Ltd.

Toronto   New York   London   Auckland   Sydney
Mexico City   New Delhi   Hong Kong   Buenos Aires

Scholastic Canada Ltd.
604 King Street West, Toronto, Ontario M5V 1E1, Canada

Scholastic Inc.
557 Broadway, new York, nY 10012, USA

Scholastic Australia Pty Limited
PO Box 579, Gosford, nSW 2250, Australia

Scholastic new Zealand Limited
Private Bag 94407, Greenmount, Auckland, new Zealand

Scholastic Ltd.
Euston House, 24 Eversholt Street, London nW1 1DB, UK

Library and Archives Canada Cataloguing in Publication
Mason, Jane B.
Back to normal / adapted by Jane Mason and Sara Hines Stephens ;
based on "Back to PCA" written by Dan Schneider and
"Time capsule" written by Steve Holland ;
based on the television series Zoey 101 created by Dan Schneider.
ISBn-13: 978-0-439-93553-1 (pbk.)
ISBn-10: 0-439-93553-9 (pbk.)
1. Boarding schools--Juvenile fiction. I. Hines-Stephens, Sarah
II. Holland, Steve III. Schneider, Dan IV. Title.
PS3613.A743B33 2006   j813'.6   C2006-905421-5

6 5 4 3 2 1   Printed in Canada   07 08 09 10 11

Back to School

Chase Matthews pedaled his bike across the Pacific Coast Academy campus. As sad as he was to see summer go, he was not at all sad to be back at PCA boarding school. He had missed the smell of the ocean. He had missed the waving palms. And he had missed his friends — especially Zoey Brooks.

Dodging arriving students and rolling luggage, Chase scanned the crowd for his buds. Everywhere people were unloading, hugging hellos, and loading up their Boogie boards with stuff. Some were heading for their dorms while others were hanging out on the lawn playing Frisbee. Speaking of — Chase snatched a flying disc out of the air before it clocked him and sent it soaring back toward its owner without slowing down. The Frisbee players gave him a nod of thanks.

In the throng, Chase finally spotted one of his friends.

"There he is." Chase slowed to a stop in front of a van to greet Logan Reese, the big-ego-on-campus and one of Chase's roommates.

"Chaaase! Whassup, buddy?" Logan slapped Chase five and thumped him on the back. He looked suitably cool in his black tank, gray camo shorts, and silver necklace. He also looked a little uptight about the boxes of stuff the moving van guys were unloading.

"Hey, man." Chase grinned and hugged Logan back. No matter how obnoxious Logan could be, Chase was glad to see him.

"So, I hear we're livin' in Rigby this year. You seen our new room yet?" Logan asked.

"Yeah, it's awesome. Um, what is all this stuff?" Chase motioned toward the piles and the three workers busily unloading an enormous amount of audio and video equipment onto the sidewalk.

Logan nodded. "Little gift from the old man," he said casually. "Specifically, a fifteen-thousand-dollar entertainment system with a forty-two-inch flat screen."

Chase watched in amazement as two guys walked past with the enormous screen. It was no secret Logan's dad was loaded. But this "little gift" was over the top!

"For our *room*?" Chase gulped. He was not complaining. He just wasn't sure how it was going to fit.

"Oh, yeah. We are *set* for video games, movies, music —" Logan ticked off the possibilities on his fingers.

"Dudes!" A familiar voice interrupted Logan's AV reverie. The boys turned to see their third roomie closing in fast with his arms spread wide.

"Michael!" Chase greeted his pal and partner in crime enthusiastically. It had been too long.

"What-up, Miguel?" Logan asked in his laid-back style.

"M'boys!" Michael grabbed Chase in a headlock hug and high-fived Logan. His trademark smile was plastered across his face. He wore a yellow shirt, accented by the bright orange messenger bag slung over his shoulder.

"So how was your summer, man?" Logan asked.

"Yeah, I've missed seeing your freakish face every day," Chase teased. But it was totally true.

"And I missed your big, bushy head." Michael reached up and patted Chase's mass of dark curls. "Hey, did it get bigger?"

Chase reached up and tousled his own hair. It had always been big, but even he had to admit it felt like it was pushing huge. "It's possible." He shrugged. "So, c'mon, catch me up on your life. Tell me stuff."

"Well, let's see. At the beginning of the summer, I started working for my dad, y'know, just like helping him out with —"

"Hey, Chase," interrupted a girl walking by. "Zoey was looking for you over behind the science center."

"Zoey?" It was all Chase needed to hear.

Michael kept talking. But from the moment Chase heard Zoey's name, Michael's voice started to fade until it was like the buzz of a mosquito in his ears. He slapped on his helmet and mounted his bike.

"Anyway, so the job was pretty lame at first, but after a couple of weeks..." Michael trailed off as he watched Chase pedal away as fast as he could. "Good talkin' to ya, man!" he called after his disappearing friend.

Riding as fast as he could, Chase crested the hill and spotted Zoey's blond head next to her roommate Nicole's dark one. The two girls were rolling and dragging their enormous bags toward the dorms.

"Zoey! Hey, Zo'!" Chase called, waving.

Zoey turned and smiled. "Chase!" she called back.

Man, she has a great smile, Chase thought. *And,*

whoa, where did those steps come from? Suddenly Chase was careening down a flight of stairs. He and his bike went flying, landing in a heap at the bottom.

"Are you okay?" Zoey dropped her bag and rushed over to help Chase up.

"I'm fine, I'm fine, I'm fine," Chase repeated, hoping it was true. "Steps." He shook his head, grumbling, and brushed himself off. He managed to make a fool of himself in front of Zoey way too often. Luckily, she didn't seem to mind.

"So, is this how we're going to start every new school year?" Zoey asked with a sly smile. She and Chase had met at the same time last year when he biked into a flagpole.

Chase blushed a little, remembering how he had been distracted the first time he saw her. Zoey looked as good as she had then in her red T-shirt and denim skirt. But when did Zoey ever look bad?

"Man, you went flying! That was awesome!" Nicole rushed over to join them. She was as enthusiastic as ever. As if Chase had totally bitten it on purpose!

"Yes," Chase said, deadpan, "it's fun to see Chase hurt himself. After dinner, I'll be stumbling, then falling off a cliff. Make sure you get good seats."

The girls cracked up.

"So, you guys back in the same dorm this year?" Chase asked.

"Unh-uh." Zoey shook her head. "We got moved to Brenner."

"Brenner? Cool dorm." Chase nodded his approval.

"And it gets cooler," Nicole burbled. "Zoey and I get a room all to ourselves!"

"What about Dana?" Chase had really been warming up to their prickly third roommate.

"She got accepted into that European exchange student thing," Zoey explained. She was excited to share a room with just Nicole, but she would miss Dana a little, too. The girl really grew on you.

"Yep. She'll be studying in Paris all semester," Nicole said, holding up her palm. "Which is awesome 'cause there's, like, no way she can irritate me all the way from France."

"Ummm . . . don't look but there's a large box with small legs coming toward us." Chase nodded to his right at the giant cardboard box staggering their way.

"Oh, that's Dustin." Nicole shrugged.

"He's going through his 'I'm a big macho man' phase." Zoey rolled her eyes before shouting to her overburdened little brother. "Hey, Dustin! You okay?"

The big box dropped to the ground with a thump and Dustin's shaggy blond head appeared over the top of it. "Yeah," he panted, leaping up to see over the box. "This is nothing." The kid heaved the box up again and continued wobbling toward the buildings.

"Well, c'mon, let's go see our new room!" Nicole held up her hands. She could barely contain herself. "I'm so excited!"

"She's excited." Zoey motioned toward her friend, who was already rushing off, leaving Chase and Zoey standing alone.

"*So* excited," Chase added. "Anyway, umm . . . I was thinkin' maybe we could meet . . . I mean, y'know, all of us could meet later at Sushi Rox . . . if you want." Sushi Rox was the Japanese restaurant on campus.

"Sure, I wanna hear about your summer," Zoey agreed. She had really missed Chase over the long break.

"Yeah, yours, too. Well, okay then. I'll, uh, call you later." Zoey had agreed to meet, so now Chase had to get going before he said something dumb.

"Good." Zoey began to walk away.

"Hey . . ." Chase called after her. "You look great." Better than he remembered even.

"You, too," Zoey called back over her shoulder.

Taking a closer look at Chase, she added, "Did your hair get bushier?"

"I've heard that," Chase admitted, running his hand through his mop. Maybe it was time for a trim.

Zoey flashed her smile one more time and picked up her bags.

Chase watched her for a moment longer, then rolled off on his bike.

Only Dustin remained, struggling with the giant wardrobe box. Groaning under the weight, he staggered and fell with the box on top of him. "Little help?" cried a muffled voice. "Boy under box!" Dustin yelled as students stepped carefully over his protruding arms and legs.

CHAPTER 2
New Room

"Will you look at our new room?" Nicole enthused. "I am in love with our new room! How much do you love our new room?" She walked around checking everything out.

"It's a cool room." Zoey had to give her that. Their dorm room was done up in purples and oranges, with geometric shelves set into the walls.

"Ahhh! We can see the tennis court from here!" Nicole shrieked, taking in the view. "That means we can watch the boys' tennis team practice! They don't always wear shirts, y'know."

"*Who* doesn't wear shirts?" A familiar squeaky voice filled Zoey and Nicole's new room, making them jump. The girls looked around before spotting a flat screen on the wall. There was a small camera mounted over it. And an unforgettable face on it, staring at them.

"Quinn?" Zoey asked, looking closer at the girl in cute glasses.

"Hi, Zoey. Hi, Nicole." Quinn waved excitedly.

"Hi. Um, why can we see you?" Nicole asked.

"I hooked up a dorm-to-dorm two-way video system so we can talk all the time," Quinn answered. She was PCA's resident genius and constantly invented things — some weirder than others.

"Wow." Zoey was not sure how she felt about having a camera in her room — and talking to Quinn *all* the time.

"And it's high-def!" Quinn said proudly. "Look at this picture quality." She moved closer to the camera. "I bet you can see right up my nose to my brain!" Quinn tipped her head back and pushed her nostrils closer to the camera.

Nicole and Zoey looked at each other. The image on the screen was a little disturbing. They were not particularly anxious to look up Quinn's nose!

"So . . . what dorm are you in?" Zoey asked, changing the subject.

"Brenner! I'm right next door!" Suddenly Quinn disappeared from the screen. A second later she reappeared in their doorway. "See?!" she exclaimed. Before Zoey and Nicole could answer, she had turned and dashed back out, braids flying. "And here I am!" she squeaked, appearing back on the monitor.

"There you are," Nicole agreed. Honestly, it was a little too much Quinn for her.

For Zoey, too. "Yeah, umm . . . so how do we turn this off?" she asked.

"Only I can turn it off — in here," Quinn spoke softly, then held up a small dark box. "Bye!" She pointed the remote at the screen, pushed a button, and the screen went dark.

"We have Quinn-a-vision," Zoey said slowly, exchanging eye rolls with Nicole.

"Apparently." Nicole looked stunned. Already her room with Zoey felt a lot less private.

Just then there was a knock at the door. Zoey turned, sure it was Quinn. But this time it was Coco, the dorm adviser. "Hey, girls."

"Hey." Zoey and Nicole smiled at the familiar face.

"Just letting you know I'll still be your dorm adviser this year," the older girl said in her raspy voice, taking a swig of bottled water.

"Oh. I thought we'd get a new DA." Zoey looked at Nicole. She didn't mean to sound disappointed. But Coco had a habit of going on and on about late-night TV, and she could be really blunt.

"Well, you thought wrong," Coco said flatly. "Hey, how do you think these pants look on me?" Coco turned around, modeling the pants from every angle.

"Umm . . ." Zoey searched for the right answer. "Great."

"Yeah, I thought so, too," Coco agreed. "Anyway, I just wanted to let you know that you guys'll be getting a new roommate either tonight or tomorrow morning."

"Wait, we thought we had this room to ourselves." Zoey was shocked.

"We don't want a new roommate," Nicole said quickly.

"Well, if wants were dreams, then wishes would fly," Coco said not so gently. There was an awkward moment of silence while they all tried to figure out what she meant. Then Coco held up a hand. "I don't know what that means," she admitted, turning. "I gotta go," she said over her shoulder. A second later she was gone.

"Okay, this is awful." Nicole started panicking immediately. "We just lost a third of our closet space to some random chick we don't even know."

"Will you chill out?" If Zoey was going to come up with a solution to their problem, she needed Nicole to get a grip.

"No! I don't want another roommate, 'cause I

already had one last year I didn't get along with, and what if this one's worse?" The terror in Nicole's voice was rising.

And Zoey had to admit Nicole had a point. Things between their old roommate, Dana, and Nicole had been so bad at the beginning of last year that Zoey had moved out for a few nights. They needed to make sure things were never that bad again. "Okay, I have an idea," Zoey said.

"Oh, thank goodness. I knew you would. Say words." Nicole waited for the idea that would soothe her frazzled nerves.

It was simple. "We'll just go to the housing office and ask to pick out our own roommate," Zoey explained.

Nicole looked relieved. "Oooh, those were good words!" If she and Zoey could pick their roommate, they'd get someone great!

CHAPTER 3

Message in a Bottle

Zoey and Nicole pushed open the swinging glass door and smiled at the woman seated behind the desk.

"Hi, is this the housing administration office?" Zoey asked, trying to sound superfriendly.

"Are you Mrs. Burvitch?" Nicole added, just to make sure.

"*Miss*," the lady corrected her sternly, eyeing both of them over her glasses. "And what do you want?" she growled.

"Umm . . . just one sec." Nicole pulled Zoey aside. "This isn't gonna work," she whispered. "She's *mean*."

"Relax." Zoey needed Nicole to stay calm — it would increase their chance of success. "We just gotta make her love us." Not too difficult, right?

Zoey turned back around and smiled again at the woman with the deadly glare. "So, Miss Burvitch . . ."

Zoey looked around. "This is such a pretty office," she said, sitting down. That was probably a huge stretch of anyone's imagination, since the room was pretty plain, with the exception of some small shelves of little bottles on the wall. But she was desperate.

"I hate it." Miss Burvitch was not fooled.

"Well" — Zoey needed to change tactics, and fast — "you deserve a better one."

"Yes," the grouchy lady agreed. "I also deserve a husband, but I haven't had a date in nine years." Miss Burvitch took off her glasses and looked at Zoey and Nicole, hard.

This was going to be tougher than Zoey thought.

"Can I help you with something?" she asked in a low voice.

"Um, yes," Nicole began nervously. "See, we just found out that we'll be getting a new roommate, and we were hoping we could give you some input —"

Miss Burvitch didn't even let Nicole finish. "Students are not allowed to choose their roommates. Roommates are chosen by me," she said, raising her eyebrows and daring them to contradict her.

This was a disaster. Zoey looked around again. She was grasping at straws. Finally her gaze fell on the shelves full of bottles. "Are those perfume bottles?"

she asked, looking more closely at the small shelves covered in tiny delicate-looking bottles.

"They are," Miss Burvitch answered. She looked at Zoey suspiciously. "Why?"

"'Cause they're so cool." Zoey walked over to get a better look. "You collect these?" Zoey tried to sound truly interested.

"They look like antiques." Nicole followed Zoey. She picked up on the new plan quickly and added her enthusiasm.

"Oh, indeed they are. In fact, my great-grandmother bought this one in 1907 while traveling through Prague." Miss Burvitch stepped over to the bottles and pointed one out. She wasn't smiling yet. But at least she was talking. They might be on to something!

"That's so interesting." Nicole nodded.

"This one," Miss Burvitch said a little reluctantly, "was hand-blown by a Norwegian woman who had only one arm."

"Ooooh." Zoey looked at Nicole. They both acted really intrigued.

"*Hand-blown,*" Nicole crooned. Miss Burvitch cracked a small smile.

Both girls' eyes were wide. Not because they didn't believe Miss Burvitch's bottle stories — because they could not believe their plan was finally starting to work!

Back in Rigby, the movers were gone and Chase and Michael were heaving Logan's giant flat-screen TV into its new home in their room while Logan hung a picture of himself on the wall.

"Entertainment system's lookin' good, boys." Logan pulled himself away from his picture to give the guys a nod of approval.

"Y'know, you could help us," Chase suggested, wondering how Logan always got out of doing work.

"Yeah, I could," Logan agreed. "But I'm gonna go get myself a smoothie. Later."

Chase and Michael shrugged. Neither of them really expected Logan to help, anyway. Grabbing a handful of cables and wire, they continued hooking up stuff.

"Hey, where do I plug in the DVD audio input?" Chase asked. He held up a wire from behind the screen.

"Um, try auxiliary one," Michael suggested as he flipped through the manual.

"'Kay . . ." The moment Chase's wire was inserted, the entire floor was filled with a horrible screeching noise. The guys covered their ears and Chase yanked the cord back out.

"Try auxiliary two," Michael suggested sheepishly. He never had been that great with technical manuals.

"You know, I'm not sure which one is prettier . . . this one from Sweden, or this one from Venezuela." Zoey pointed at two lovely small bottles.

"Who can decide?" Nicole cooed with her hands up in surrender.

"Let's call it a tie!" Miss Burvitch was actually smiling a real smile now. She looked positively tickled to be stuck with such a problem — and such a pair of like-minded admirers!

"Yay!" Nicole clapped.

"So . . ." Zoey was ready to change the subject. She hoped the housing administrator would now be open to their little suggestion.

"Hmmm?" Miss Burvitch sounded like she had just awakened from a wonderful dream.

"Well, we were just feeling a little nervous about this whole new roommate situation. . . ." Zoey spoke slowly. She didn't want to push too hard.

"Yeah, I mean, don't you think maybe you could let us . . ." Nicole began.

"*Choose* who we'll live with?" Zoey finished.

"Well . . ." Miss Burvitch raised her eyebrows again. "That really goes against my policy."

"But . . ." Zoey could feel her beginning to cave. There just had to be a "but."

"But I think we can make an exception." Miss Burvitch made her way back to her desk.

"Really?"

"That's so awesome!" Zoey and Nicole looked at each other excitedly.

"Just let me bring up your dorm on my computer and then we'll look through the list of girls who've yet to be assigned." Miss Burvitch opened her laptop and slipped her glasses back onto her nose.

"That would be so great," Zoey said gratefully.

"You are the best." Nicole thumped the wall, accidentally knocking the clear shelves holding the entire bottle collection. They clattered to the ground, shattering all of the antique glass.

Miss Burvitch clutched her chest. She looked like she had just lost a beloved friend or relative.

For a moment Nicole was speechless. "Um . . . your wall unit's loose," she said lamely.

Miss Burvitch did not say a word. Like a zombie, she walked toward the disaster with bits of glass crunching under her heels.

Zoey scrambled to do a little damage control. "Okay, obviously a very bad thing just happened . . . so, if you could just let us pick out our roommate —"

"Out!" Miss Burvitch erupted, pointing at the door. She didn't have to ask twice. There was nothing Nicole and Zoey could do — except run!

Get the Party Started!

The music was thumpin' and the party was raging in Rigby. Logan's new room of technology was up and running. It was totally wicked . . . as long as you didn't want to get your homework done.

"What the —" Michael walked into his dorm room and did a double take. Kids were dancing. Kids were drinking soda. Kids were watching aliens flying around a giant screen and getting blown up. Dustin was completely engrossed in a video game on the flat screen.

It took Michael a minute to spot Chase in the middle of the chaos typing away on his laptop. "Chase . . . *Chase!*" Michael yelled over the noise, trying to get his friend's attention. Finally Chase looked up.

"Hey!" Chase yelled.

"Why are all these people here?" Michael bellowed as the sound of an explosion rocked the room.

"To check out Logan's entertainment system," Chase shouted back.

"Well, it's too loud —" Michael was interrupted again by explosions and technotronic beeps.

"What?" Chase couldn't hear a word. The music was blasting. It was as intense as a rock concert!

"I said it's too . . ." Michael shook his head and walked over to Logan. "It's too . . ." Logan could not hear a word, either, but that might have been because he was talking to a girl. "Dude . . . dude . . . *dude!*" Michael had to scream to get Logan's attention.

"What?" Logan whipped around, annoyed at the interruption. The girl slipped away.

"Will ya turn that down a little?" Michael asked, motioning toward the sound system.

"Huh?" Logan looked puzzled. What was the problem?

"I said . . . *could you turn that down a little*?!" Michael shouted as loudly as he could.

"Oh." Logan finally heard him. "No." He shook his head and walked away to see how Dustin was doing with his game.

"I'm gonna get ya!" Dustin yelled at the screen, totally absorbed in his game and oblivious to everything else around him. "Here come the torpedoes!" Dustin hit the button on his controls, launching the weapons and landing a hit. *BOOM!*

"Whoa! Level forty-seven, not bad," Logan said, noting the little guy's score. He took a seat so he could enjoy the action.

"Not bad? I'm awesome!" Dustin was pumped.

"Maybe, but this game's got a hundred levels." Logan nudged Dustin's shoulder. "There's still a long way to go."

"Dude." Dustin shrugged him off. "I'm ten years old. I got time." Dustin launched into the next level. Around him, the party continued to rage.

". . . I'm telling you, you really should floss twice a day." Nicole was going off on one of her dental hygiene tangents when she and Zoey got back to their room. They had both decided to put the whole Miss Burvitch episode behind them and deal with whatever roommate they got. But that was before they actually met her. . . .

When they stepped inside their room they immediately sensed that things were different. For one thing, there were candles burning on every surface. And a girl with white spiky hair, a nose ring, and spooky black goth clothes was sitting cross-legged on the floor. She was also surrounded by candles and was moving her arms in wide circles.

"Hi." Zoey tried not to sound too weirded out. "Do we know you?" she asked uncertainly.

"No," the girl answered impatiently, continuing to wave her arms. She wore at least a dozen silver necklaces around her neck.

"Well." It was Nicole's turn. "Do you wanna tell us why you're sitting in the middle of our —?"

"Shhh," the spooky girl shushed Nicole. "I'm trying to talk to the dead." She looked annoyed, as if this should be obvious.

Zoey and Nicole exchanged concerned looks. What was going on?

"Okay, who *are* you?" Zoey tried again, this time getting right to the point.

"Lola," the girl replied, her silver jewelry swaying. She did not smile. Her dark-stained lips looked like they were in a permanent frown. "I'm your new roommate," she said ominously.

Nicole's jaw dropped. Zoey's eyes grew wide. Lola started to chant toward the heavens in a really eerie way.

This was scarier than Zoey and Nicole could have ever imagined. Their new roommate was some kind of weirdo from the dark side!

CHAPTER 5

Roommate Troubles

Zoey stared at the girl sitting on the floor. Last year she and Nicole had had to deal with grumpy Dana, who actually turned out to be pretty nice once you got to know her. This year they got . . . freaky girl. Suddenly Dana seemed like the greatest roommate in the world.

Lola got to her feet. One by one, she picked up a candle and blew it out with a heavy puff of air. Her steps were heavy and plodding, almost like she *was* one of the dead.

Trying to stay calm, Zoey watched Lola move around the room. "So . . ." Zoey said, not sure what to say. "You're our new roommate."

"Yep," Lola said casually, as if she were like any other roommate at PCA. She carefully set a white candle down on a side table.

Nicole stared at the artwork on the walls. It was . . . scary. She felt like she was in a haunted house! "I see you've put some of your . . . artwork . . . up already." She shivered as she examined the paintings.

Lola looked around the room with satisfaction. "Oh, yeah. You like 'em?" she asked, smiling darkly.

Zoey stared at the paintings on the wall. One was bloodred with black branchy-looking brush marks. Another was putrid green with a giant pink blob in the middle. Just looking at them sent shivers down her spine. But she didn't want to be rude, no matter how bizarre her new roommate was. "Ummm . . . they're pretty. . . ." Zoey mumbled.

Nicole leaned in close to Zoey. "Disturbing," she finished, looking like she'd swallowed something rotten. It was exactly what Zoey was thinking.

"Thanks," Lola said proudly. "I painted this one myself." She pointed to a particularly weird-looking painting. "That's my cat."

"That's your cat?" Zoey asked in disbelief. It looked more like her breakfast cereal after it had sat for several hours.

"Yes," Lola confirmed, walking over to the mini fridge. "After the accident," she added in a sinister voice.

Zoey shot Nicole an alarmed look. But she had to

keep her cool. If Lola was their roommate, they had to find a way to all get along. "So, is this the first time you've ever gone to a boarding school?" she asked, trying to sound welcoming.

Lola took a carton of eggs out of the fridge. "Nah," she said, waving her hand. "Last year I went to one in upstate New York." She set the carton of eggs down on top of a table next to a tall glass. Opening the carton, she took out an egg and cracked it. *Glub!* The egg slipped into the glass.

"And why'd you leave?" Nicole asked nervously, wishing the girl had stayed. Lola really was making Dana look like roommate perfection.

Lola cracked another egg into the glass. "Well, legally I'm not supposed to talk about it," she said conspiratorially. "But let's just say that a certain teacher *fell* down the stairs, no matter what anyone says."

Nicole's eyes widened. This girl was not only freaky, she was dangerous! She leaned in toward Zoey again. "She pushed her teacher down the stairs!" she whispered frantically.

"*Shhhh,*" Zoey shushed her. The last thing they wanted was for Lola to think they were afraid of her . . . even if they were, a little. "Well, anyway," she said kind of loudly. "I'm Zoey."

"Nicole," Nicole added, trying to keep her voice from shaking.

Lola cracked a third egg into the glass. She eyed the girls from under her spiky bangs. Then she picked up the glass of eggs and gulped it down as if it were freshly squeezed orange juice. Setting the glass down with a flourish, she smacked her lips loudly.

Zoey and Nicole stared, totally grossed out. Their new roommate just got even freakier.

The next day Zoey and Nicole were hanging out studying with Quinn, Chase, and Michael. Zoey filled them in on their weirdo roommate between math problems.

"She drank eggs?" Chase asked, making a face and shaking his curly head.

"*Raw* eggs," Zoey said, plucking grapes from the large bunch sitting in front of her.

"Okay, weird," Chase admitted.

"*Yeah,*" Nicole said emphatically. She still could not believe that she and Zoey were stuck with such a creepy roommate. Nicole thought of herself as a nice, normal person who just wanted to do regular teenage stuff. What had she done to deserve this?

Quinn pushed her square eyeglass frames high on

her nose. "Actually, raw eggs are an excellent source of protein, and as long as they're fresh and free from salmonella, they're a fairly decent high-energy snack," she explained with a smile. Although she personally didn't eat raw eggs on a regular basis, there were plenty of scientific reasons for doing so.

"She also talks to the dead," Zoey said flatly, her arms crossed in front of her on the table. Nobody was going to try and tell her that her new roommate was normal.

Quinn shuddered, the small feathers at the ends of her braids quivering slightly. "Okay, weird," she agreed.

"Well, I'd still rather live with her than with Logan," Michael said, sounding exasperated. He turned a page in his textbook and tried to get the thudding sound of Logan's stereo out of his head. It felt like it was in there permanently!

"Word," Chase said, clutching his pencil tightly.

Michael shot him a look.

"Sorry," he added sheepishly.

Zoey and Nicole exchanged glances. What was that about?

"So, Logan still won't turn off his billion-dollar

entertainment system?" Nicole asked. She had to agree that having Logan for a roommate would be a bummer, even without the irritating blaring stereo.

"No," Chase said, clearly annoyed.

"Man, he had that thing blastin' till three in the morning. I didn't get any sleep," Michael complained. "And when I don't get enough sleep, I get cranky."

Chase nodded, making his curls bob. "He does. Watch this. What's up, Michael?" he said, giving his friend an ultrafriendly wave.

Michael glared. "Get outta my face," he growled.

"See that?" Chase said, pointing at Michael's annoyed expression.

"Cranky," Michael confirmed with a smile. They were just playacting. But Logan and his stereo system were no joke. In fact, Michael was about ready to throw Logan's stereo system out the window, no matter how much it cost.

"So, what are you gonna do about Lola?" Chase asked, changing the subject. Just the thought of that blaring stereo made his head hurt. Besides, if he could help Zoey out with her roommate situation, he'd make her happy. And making Zoey happy was a good thing.

"I'll tell ya what we're gonna do," Nicole said, her face full of determination. Then she suddenly looked stumped. "What are we gonna do?" she asked, turning to Zoey.

Zoey was ready for this. "Well, after school I think we should just talk to her and let her know that if she wants to be all weird, fine . . . but she can't be weird in *our* room." She plucked another juicy grape off the bunch and popped it into her mouth. How hard could it be?

"Right," Nicole agreed, feeling relieved. Zoey always knew what to do. It was one of the best things about her.

"Totally," Zoey said, sounding more convinced than she suddenly felt. There was something a little off about her plan, something she couldn't put her finger on. But since she didn't have a better idea, she was going to go with it.

Nicole felt worry creep up on her again. "You'll do all the talking, right?" she asked Zoey a little nervously.

"Sure," Zoey agreed. She'd been expecting that. Confrontation was not Nicole's strong suit.

"Oh, thank you," Nicole said, letting out a big breath of air.

A little while later, Zoey and Nicole walked into their room. Lola was sitting at a table in the corner with her back to them.

"Lola, we want to talk to you," Zoey said matter-of-factly.

Lola mumbled something, but Zoey couldn't understand a word. She sounded like her mouth was full of toothpaste, or food, or something.

"Huh?" Zoey asked.

"What are you doing?" Nicole asked, taking a step forward.

Lola spun around in her swivel chair. She had a big metal clamp in her mouth and a long metal instrument with a circle at the end in the other. She removed the clamp and smiled up at Zoey and Nicole.

"I'm piercing my tongue," she announced.

"Piercing your tongue?" Zoey repeated, trying not to sound too disgusted.

"In our room?" Nicole added, putting her hand on her chest. Disgusting!

Lola ignored them. Then her face lit up like she'd just gotten a great idea. "Hey, could one of you hold this metal thing while I put the needle through?" she asked cheerfully.

Zoey shot Nicole a "this is out of control" look.

"C'mon, Nicole?" Lola prodded.

"Noooo!" Nicole practically shrieked. "I don't wanna get tongue blood on me!"

"Baby," Lola teased.

Zoey folded her arms across her chest. "Look, if you have to do this, fine, but could you do it somewhere else, please?"

Lola's cheerful expression disappeared in an instant. "Okay, look," she said, walking toward them. "This is my room just as much as it's yours. And if I wanna shove a needle through my tongue I will, right here, in *my* room."

She stuck her tongue out and placed the circle on top of it, as if showing where the hole would go. "Ahhhh!" she said loudly.

All of a sudden Zoey understood what was wrong with her plan. Lola was right. It wasn't just her and Nicole's room. It was Lola's room, too. She still thought Lola was weird. She still thought Lola did freaky stuff. But Lola had every right to do freaky stuff in her own room — no matter how annoying it was.

"Oh, yeah?" Nicole shot back. "Well . . . Zoey's got something to say about that." She gave Zoey a little slap on the shoulder. "Go, Zo'." She eyed Lola warily while she waited for Zoey to pipe up and tell the girl off.

Zoey looked at Nicole, then at Lola. Without saying anything to either of them, she turned on her heels and stormed out of the room.

Nicole stood there feeling kind of stupid. What happened? Zoey was supposed to tell Lola off! "Um . . . I have to go get my . . . thing. . . ." she babbled, taking a step backward. ". . . In the thing," she finished lamely. Then she turned and raced out the door. She had to find Zoey!

Zoey was standing outside the dorm, fuming in the California sunshine. Nicole rushed up to her. "Okay, not to be critical, but you weren't very tough with her," she said.

Zoey glared. "Well, what do you want me to say?" she said, totally exasperated. "She's kinda right."

"What?" Nicole asked, dumbfounded.

"It *is* her room, just as much as it's ours," Zoey explained. The truth was painful.

Nicole was silent for a second. This was an interesting point. Interesting, and annoying. "So that gives her the right to freak us out all the time?" she asked, trying not to think about the ways in which Lola could do exactly that.

"I dunno," Zoey admitted. This was so frustrating!

"Well, you gotta figure this out!" Nicole said. Zoey was definitely the figure-outer.

Zoey scowled. She'd always thought of herself as a person of action. But sometimes she wanted someone *else* to take action. "Why do I always have to figure everything out?" she asked huffily.

"'Cause that's how it works. I point out problems and issues, and you fix 'em. It's a good system and I don't see it changing anytime soon," Nicole said matter-of-factly.

Zoey had to admit it was true. She was the one who got the girls accepted on the basketball team. She was the one who came up with a solution when Dana and Nicole were fighting the year before. She even managed to get even with Stacy, a senior who stole her backpack idea.

Zoey let out a long sigh. "All right," she agreed. "But this one's not so easy — this one might take some time to fix."

Nicole looked at their dorm and shuddered. "Well, until you do, I don't think I wanna sleep in there."

"I don't, either," Zoey admitted.

Just then the dorm door opened and Lola leaned out. "Hey, would you guys look and tell me if the hole goes all the way through?" she asked casually.

"Nope," Nicole said.

"Not really," Zoey said, wincing. Gross!

CHAPTER 6

Camp Out

Over in Rigby, Logan's party was going full blast. Dustin still sat in front of the giant flat-screen TV, madly punching the buttons on the video control clutched tightly in his hand. Logan was working the crowd, making sure everyone was having a good time and admiring his new entertainment system. Over in the corner, Michael and Chase were trying to study.

"Alabama," Michael practically shouted, leaning in so close to Chase he could almost count his cavities. They were doing geography.

"Uh, capital would be Montgomery," Chase yelled, nodding. He knew the answer was right.

"What?" Michael asked.

"Montgomery," Chase repeated even louder.

"Right," Michael said, finally getting it. "Okay,

hush . . ." It was so hard to think over the noise. "Tennessee."

"Memphis."

"No, Nashville," Michael corrected, wincing from the noise.

"What?" Chase yelled.

"Nashville!"

Chase wrinkled his forehead in confusion. "Who's Phil?" he yelled to his friend.

Michael groaned. This was impossible! "I can't take this!" he shouted, slamming his book shut and kicking back his chair. He stalked up to Logan, who was standing over Dustin, watching the kid's video game progress.

"Give me that remote," Michael demanded, trying to grab it right out of Logan's hand. He wasn't usually so pushy, but the situation called for desperate measures.

Logan looked at Michael as if he were a bug. "No," he refused. He yanked his arm away from his roommate. "And stop distracting us," he added hotly. "The kid's on fire!" He pumped his fist in the air and gestured to Dustin, who looked like a video game zombie. "What level you at?" he asked.

"Seventy-nine!" Dustin replied, staring at the screen and frantically pushing buttons. "Wait . . . eighty!"

"Yes!" Logan cheered. A bunch of partygoers pumped their fists in the air.

By now Chase had joined them. He stared Logan down. Enough was enough. "At least turn the sound down!" It was somewhere between an order and a whimper.

Logan rolled his eyes. As if. "Why don't ya turn your mouth down?" he taunted. What was wrong with these guys? Didn't they know a good time when it was right in their faces?

"That's it!" Chase said. He couldn't believe what a jerk Logan was being. The guy had an ego bigger than the dorm and could be kind of insensitive. But he'd never been this annoying for this long. "We're not sleeping here." Chase hoped it would sound like a threat.

"Yeah!" Michael agreed.

Unfortunately, Logan could not have cared less. "Yeah?" he asked, scoffing. "Then where are you gonna sleep?"

Michael looked over at Chase. The dude had a point. And he had no answer. "Where are we gonna sleep?" he echoed.

Chase was quiet for a minute, thinking. Where on campus could a couple of exiled guys spend the night?

An hour later Chase was rolling around inside a tent approximately ten feet away from Michael, who was inside his own tent. They'd pitched them right in the middle of a PCA quad.

Chase curled up in his yellow sleeping bag and breathed in the night air. It was so peaceful out here, and much, much quieter. Except for the crickets, there was no sound at all.

"Chase," Michael called.

Chase didn't reply. He was too busy soaking in the quiet, or trying to.

"Chase. Chase!" Michael wouldn't give up.

Chase rolled over and popped his head out of the tent. "What?" he asked, trying not to sound exasperated. He had a feeling Michael hadn't done much camping before. It took him forever to pitch his tent.

"I don't like being alone in here," Michael said.

Chase rolled his eyes. It wasn't like they were deep in the forest or anything. "Just go to sleep," he suggested.

"I've been trying!" Michael insisted.

"Try harder," Chase said. The last thing he needed was for Michael to keep him up all night!

Chase slipped back inside his tent and climbed

back into his sleeping bag. He was just dozing off when his cell phone rang. Michael. Again. Annoyed, he picked up the call. "Hello?" he greeted.

"There's a bug in my tent!" Michael complained. He sounded a little wigged.

"So kill it," Chase suggested calmly.

"No!" Michael sounded offended.

"Why not?" he asked.

"What if he has a family?" Michael asked, sitting up. This was kind of serious.

"It's a bug!" Chase replied. Who was Michael kidding?

"Bugs have children," Michael said gravely.

Chase considered this. It was possible, he supposed. "Well, maybe he's a mean, horrible bug that all the other bugs hate and you'll be a hero for taking his life."

"Wait!" Michael shouted.

Chase groaned inwardly. What now? "What?"

"I hear something outside my tent," he said.

"It's probably just the wind," Chase said reasonably.

"What if it's a bear?" Michael's voice was full of panic.

"Ask him to step on the bug," Chase grumbled.

This was almost as bad as having to deal with Logan's stupid stereo!

Michael listened carefully. There was definitely something out there. "I'm going to investigate," he told Chase.

Anything to get you off the phone! Chase thought. Michael was a great friend, but right now he was driving Chase nuts. Chase already had one irritating roommate. He didn't need another one!

Michael picked up his giant green flashlight. It would provide some protection, at least. Whatever was out there, it looked . . . big! He could see its shadow moving along his tent wall.

Flipping his phone shut, he crawled the rest of the way out of his sleeping bag. This was a time for courage. He paused just inside his tent door and took a deep breath. And then . . .

"Ahhhhhh!" he shouted, bursting into the night.

"Ahhhhhh!" Zoey and Nicole jumped back, totally freaked out. A bright light shone in their eyes. They were being attacked!

Michael was so busy screaming and flailing his arms that he didn't see who was outside his tent. "Ahhhhhh!" he shrieked again.

Chase emerged from his tent, adding his voice to

the screaming. There were obviously a bunch of crazy people loose on campus!

Suddenly Michael stopped and stared. The "bear" in front of him was really just Nicole and Zoey. He'd gotten freaked out by a couple of girls! "Man!" he said, panting. "You almost made me wet my pants!"

"You're the one who jumped out at us, waving your giant flashlight!" Zoey shot back, gasping for breath. They'd just been walking along when Michael came after them.

"Well, you scared me!" Michael protested.

"Uh, ditto!" Nicole said a little hotly. *Sheesh!*

"What are you guys doin' here?" Chase asked. He was thrilled to see Zoey at *any* time. But he hadn't been expecting to see her or Nicole here in the middle of the night.

"We *tried* to find you at your dorm," Zoey said pointedly. It wasn't their fault the guys were sleeping outside in tents. Or that Michael freaked out and attacked them!

"And Logan said you were sleeping outside in a tent." Nicole gestured to the pair of tents pitched on the grass.

"So we've been walking around for half an hour

trying to find you," Zoey said. She was feeling a little fed up. First wacky Lola and then a wild goose chase.

"Yeah. We wanna ask a favor," Nicole explained, getting straight to the point.

"What?" Chase asked. There wasn't much he wouldn't do for Zoey . . . or Nicole.

"Can we use one of your tents?" Zoey asked, a little sheepishly.

"Why?" Michael wanted further explanation. It wasn't exactly normal for PCA students to crash in the campus's great outdoors.

"'Cause we are not sleeping in the same room with freaky Lola." Nicole said emphatically, gesturing with her arm. There was no way.

"I thought you were gonna work that out," Chase said. It was unusual for Zoey not to follow through on a plan. What had happened?

"Well, we didn't," Zoey said flatly. She didn't really want to go into the details. It was late, she was tired, and their new roommate was making her crazy! "So can we use one of these tents?"

"Please?" Nicole added.

Chase shrugged. "Sure, go for it," he said.

Michael saw his chance — the chance to sleep in a

bug-free tent — and took it. "Take that one," he said, pointing to his tent.

Nicole beamed. Finally, a place to sleep! "Yay! C'mon, Zo'." She pulled her friend into their home away from home. But a few seconds later a pair of earsplitting screams echoed in the night air. The tent walls shook violently, as if they were in an earthquake.

"Kill it!"

"You kill it!"

"Move!"

"Ow!"

"Sorry!"

"Where'd it go?"

"There it is!"

"Get it!"

Nicole and Zoey burst out of the tent like they were escaping a monster. A second later Michael rushed through his tent door, still holding his giant flashlight. Chase rolled out a second later, somersault style.

"What?" Chase asked the girls.

"What happened?" Michael added, though he had a pretty good idea already.

"There's a ginormous bug in there!" Zoey said, wiping at her arms in case it was still crawling on her. Nicole was swatting at her arms and legs frantically.

"Really?" Michael pretended to be surprised.

Zoey shook her head. She'd had enough. "Okay, you know what? That's it," she said.

"Right!" Nicole agreed. Except she had no idea what she was agreeing to. "What do you mean?" she asked, looking for clarification.

"We were here way before this Lola girl and we are not gonna let her drive us out of our own dorm!" Zoey said determinedly.

"Good!" Nicole smiled. Finally, Zoey was ready to take action! The only problem was, taking action against Lola wasn't exactly easy. "What are you gonna do?" she prodded.

Zoey sighed. She was a little tired of taking care of everything, even if it was their system. "We are gonna go tell that freaky chick to either start acting like a person or move back to Weird Town!"

"Yeah!" Nicole echoed.

Zoey turned on her heel and hoofed it toward her dorm. But it only took a second to realize that Nicole was not with her. Turning around, she grabbed Nicole by the arm and pulled her toward Brenner. They had to act now, before she lost her nerve. And she needed Nicole by her side for moral support.

"Good luck!" Chase called after them. He gazed at

Michael as a wave of sleepiness washed over him. "I'm goin' back to sleep," he told his friend.

Michael stood alone on the quad. He looked at his tent. He looked at Chase's tent. Then he crawled into Chase's tent.

"Go sleep in *your* tent," Chase griped.

"There's a bug in there!" Michael protested.

Chase wasn't hearing it. "Out!" he ordered, raising a hand to point to the door.

Michael crawled out of Chase's tent. He raised his flashlight in the air. He stepped into his own tent. "Ahhhhh!" he shrieked. The tent walls shook like mad yet again.

CHAPTER 7

Game Over

Lola relaxed on the sofa in her room. She was practically lying down, shoes off, kickin' it while she chatted on the phone. Her roommates were nowhere in sight.

"No, it's true . . . they totally bought it. You should see me!" she bragged to her friend. Her amazing act was totally worth telling. It wasn't every day that she pulled off a stunt like this. What a couple of gullible sissies!

Running her fingers through her long, dark, pink-streaked hair, Lola was so busy talking she didn't hear the door open. Or Nicole and Zoey step inside.

"I've been wearing, like, all black clothes and I made my hair look obnoxious . . . yeah, fake nose ring. I'm serious!"

Zoey narrowed her eyes at the girl sitting on the sofa. Was this some kind of joke?

"Yeah, they're so freaked out they won't even sleep in the same room as me! Uh-huh. I'm telling you, I will have my first Oscar by my nineteenth birthday. Yeah, ooooh, and tomorrow . . ."

Okay, she got it. Lola was not a freak, she was a liar! And a game player! And Zoey Brooks did not appreciate being played with. Furious, Zoey slammed the door, hard.

Startled, Lola whipped around to see her roommates glaring at her. Uh-oh. "Bye!" she said into the phone, hanging up as fast as she could.

She grabbed her wig off the coffee table and stuck it on her head. "Hello," she said in her ominous voice.

"Drop it, Lola," Zoey said flatly, crossing the room in a few steady strides. She was not going to be messed with for one minute longer.

"If that is your real name," Nicole added testily, coming up beside Zoey. Who did this girl think she was? It was not okay to lie to your roommates!

"'Cause that's sure not your real hair," Zoey said.

Lola gulped and pulled off her wig. "Hiii," she said, trying to sound friendly. If the goth act was up, maybe she could win them over with kindness.

"Okay, so this whole thing was just an act?" Zoey still couldn't believe it. Who did stuff like that?

"Uh-huh," Lola admitted with a shrug.

"Why?" Nicole asked.

"'Cause I'm an actress," Lola said. Acting was what she did, period. It was in her blood.

"Yeah?" Zoey said, folding her arms across her chest and waiting. This had better be good. "Keep talking."

"This was the perfect acting exercise," Lola told them. "I got to play a character completely different from myself and see if people believed it."

Nicole looked confused. "You following this?" she asked Zoey.

"Nope," Zoey replied. She was, kinda. But it was all too weird and conniving.

Lola beamed. "Think about it. How many times do you get to start at a new school where not even one person knows who you really are?" It had all been so perfect!

"Um, can we not make this a quiz?" Nicole asked. It was hard enough to figure out as it was!

"Just get to the point," Zoey said, stepping forward. This was almost as annoying as the weird-girl act.

"Look, I knew I was a good actress, but now I know I'm awesome! 'Cause I totally made you guys think I was some kinda freak chick!" Lola was practically tingling from her acting success.

"You *are* a freak chick! Just for *doing* that!" Zoey said, totally exasperated.

"Yeah, who pretends she's a psychopath just to see if she can pull it off?" Nicole asked, finally getting it — and getting annoyed all at once.

"Me!" Lola chortled. Her face was lit up like a birthday cake. "How great am I?"

Zoey gave Lola a disgusted look. Unbelievable!

The sounds coming from Logan's room were deafening. It was a never-ending party fest right on the PCA campus. Dustin was still glued to his seat, holding the remote control for the video game he was playing. And he was still on fire.

"Level ninety-eight!" he cackled a little crazily.

"Ninety-eight!" onlookers cheered. "Go, kid!"

Michael and Chase stumbled through the door looking a little bleary but determined to take back their room.

"Hey, it's my roomies!" Logan greeted them, as if he'd known they'd be back. He was glad to see them. They'd obviously realized that his entertainment system was almost as great as he was. But he couldn't help rubbing it in a little. "I thought you guys were gonna crash in a tent somewhere."

Michael shook his head. "Nah. We thought about it, and we decided we want to party with you." He put his arm around Logan and rocked him back and forth a couple of times.

Chase nodded. "Yeah, let's crank that bad boy up!" he said excitedly, taking the giant remote control out of Logan's hand. He hit the volume-up button eight times.

"Hey!" Logan objected. "That's a little *too* loud."

Michael shook his head. They were just getting it right! "No, it's cool!" he insisted. "Louder, man!" he told Chase.

Across the room, Dustin's fingers were moving as fast as lightning. "Level ninety-nine!" he shouted. He was almost there. He could taste level one hundred!

Chase hit the volume button again. The stereo was on full blast.

Logan put his hands over his ears. "Whoa, turn it down!" he begged.

Chase just smiled calmly. "No way, man!" he refused. Finally, he was the one in control.

Dustin was frantic. He could barely keep up! "I'm gonna do it!" he shouted. "I'm gonna hit level one hundred!"

"Crank up the bass!" Michael shouted.

Chase put the bass all the way up. *Ba-boom! Ba-*

boom! The thudding was so loud, the room started to shake.

"Turn it down!" Logan yelled. He looked like the noise was making his head throb.

"Why?" Chase asked innocently. Logan liked loud music, didn't he?

Suddenly a lamp slipped off a table and crashed to the floor. A picture of Logan fell off the wall. All the lights in the room began to flicker.

Then all the lights in Rigby flickered . . . and went out altogether. Everyone in Logan's room — and the entire dorm — was in complete darkness.

"G'night, Michael," Chase said cheerfully.

"Sleep tight, Chase," Michael replied.

There was a moment of silence. And then . . .

"So . . . close," Dustin said, sounding utterly defeated.

Logan fumed in the darkness. The party was just getting good! Now there was nothing, and his stereo might be broken! "You guys are the worst," he announced.

CHAPTER 8

Payback

Lola strolled into her room carrying her makeup bag. Now that she didn't have to be a goth girl, she was dressed in a colorful outfit complete with chunky necklaces and a big red beret. "Mornin', ladies," she greeted Zoey and Nicole. "Got my makeup done in a record thirty-four minutes. You guys wanna get some breakfast before class?"

"Sure," Zoey agreed.

"Let's go." Nicole was ready, too.

Zoey looked at Nicole. "Wait a minute, is that my shirt?" she asked accusingly.

Nicole suddenly looked nervous. "Um, yeah, but listen —"

Zoey ignored her plea. "You know how I feel about you borrowing my clothes!" She sounded totally teed.

"Well, what are you gonna do about it?" Nicole retorted snottily.

"Guys!" Lola interrupted, trying to diffuse the situation.

Zoey stared at Nicole, hard. "Okay, you're done," she announced. Half a second later she tackled Nicole, taking her to the carpet. But Nicole wasn't going down without a fight. They kicked and slapped and punched each other, writhing around on the floor like a couple of pro wrestlers.

"You guys! Stop it!" Lola shrieked. This was really getting out of control, and she had no idea what to do. Should she go look for Coco? Break it up herself? "Are you insane? Quit it! You're gonna kill each other!"

All of a sudden Zoey and Nicole rolled onto their backs, laughing like crazy.

"Okay, what is going on?" Lola asked, confused and annoyed.

Zoey got to her feet and offered a hand to Nicole. They both straightened their clothes and stood before Lola, grinning.

"We were just acting," Zoey explained cheerfully.

"Yeah. We just wanted to see if we could pull it off." Nicole beamed at Zoey. "You're good," she complimented.

"You, too," Zoey replied. She gave Lola a "right back atcha" look, then walked out the door with Nicole.

Lola stood alone in the center of the room, dumbfounded. She'd been beaten at her own game. She was still contemplating this development when Zoey and Nicole stuck their heads back through the door.

"Hey," Nicole called.

"You coming to breakfast or what?" Zoey added. Now that they'd evened the score, she was ready to get to know her new roommate. Maybe under all that acting stuff she was a great girl.

Lola smiled and followed her roommates out the door.

Back in the Day

When Zoey walked into Mr. Bender's class with Lola a few days later, the guys were already there, bent over a book and cracking up.

"Hey," Zoey greeted them. She took off her pack and slid into her seat beside Chase.

"Hey."

"'Sup."

"Yo."

The boys barely looked up. They were too busy laughing.

"What are you guys giggling about?" Zoey had to know. She leaned in closer to try and catch a glimpse.

"Oh," Chase said, finally noticing the girls, "just this old PCA yearbook." He held the book up higher so everyone could see.

"It's, like, from twenty years ago," Logan explained,

turning a page and pointing at a picture of kids on campus. "Whoa, check out this dude's pants." The "dude" was wearing bright yellow baggy jogging pants with a matching jacket.

"What-up with the puffy pants?" Chase could not imagine putting on an outfit that loose and bright . . . ever. The guy looked like a bumblebee.

Zoey held back a laugh as she scanned the other photos on the page. The fashions *were* pretty bad. And the clothes were just one part of it. "Oh wow! Look at that teacher's giant hair." She pointed out a teacher whose mane made Chase's bushy head look like a crew cut.

Behind Logan, Michael poked his finger at another fashion faux pas. "Who wears a neon jacket?" he asked, stunned.

"Why are everyone's clothes so baggy?" Lola wanted to know. Nothing fit right. Didn't anyone try stuff on in the eighties?

The crew was so busy laughing that they didn't notice Mr. Bender come into the room. "Whatcha guys got there?" the teacher asked.

"An old PCA yearbook," Zoey answered.

"From like way back in the eighties," Chase explained.

Lola crossed her arms over her black T-shirt and smirked. "It looks like PCA used to be a school for geeks and losers," she announced.

"Hey," Mr. Bender said, taking a closer look. "You know what? That's *my* old yearbook." He looked a little amused, and offended.

"Whoops." Lola's big silver disk earrings dangled over her shoulders. She hadn't meant to insult Mr. Bender. For a teacher, Bender was pretty cool.

"You went to PCA?" Zoey had no idea.

"Yeah, for like six years." Mr. Bender nodded. He sounded kind of proud, like going to PCA was something he loved.

"Okay, wait a minute!" Logan turned the book around so it faced Mr. Bender, then pointed at a picture of a kid with large reddish hair, even larger glasses, and a goofy smile. "Is this *you* with the big round freakish glasses?"

Mr. Bender shook his finger at the book and then at the kids, but it was clear he was trying not to laugh. "Okay, those glasses were very fashionable back in the day," he insisted.

"That's you?" Michael could not believe his eyes. He took a closer look at the photo, at the live Bender in front of him, and back at the photo. "That's *you*!" Michael laughed loudly for a few seconds but quickly reeled it in when he caught the look on Mr. Bender's face. He suddenly felt a little nervous. "You were very handsome," he added, trying to sound sincere.

Zoey and the rest of the kids fought back their giggles. The photo of Mr. Bender was hilarious.

"Yeah, just wait," Bender said, planting his hands on his hips. He almost sounded bent out of shape. But Mr. Bender was one of the coolest teachers at PCA, so he wasn't going to freak out or anything. Still, he had to make his point. "I bet in twenty years a bunch of PCA students will be looking at your guys' yearbook, making fun of what you're wearing right now."

"I doubt it." Lola looked down, admiring her black V-neck top with its cute heart print.

Suddenly Chase had a thought. "Hey, if PCA students are looking at our yearbook twenty years from now, you think they'll wonder what we were like?" Chase asked aloud. It was kind of a cool concept.

"Probably." Michael nodded.

Zoey was quiet, thinking. She was pretty positive that the PCA students in the future would be curious about their predecessors. It gave Zoey an idea. "Oooh, you know what'd be cool?" she said as the idea took shape in her mind.

"Being married to Orlando Bloom?" Lola offered.

"No," Zoey answered. Then after thinking about it for a second, she had to give it to Lola. "Well, yeah." But that had not been what she was thinking. "What if we made a time capsule?" she suggested.

"Interesting." Chase was liking this idea. Zoey was always coming up with good ones, and this was no exception.

"What's a time capsule?" Logan asked. He'd heard the phrase before but had no idea what it meant.

"It's a container that you put things in, then bury. And sometime in the future, other people open it up and take a look," Mr. Bender explained.

"Cool," Lola said with a nod. Maybe not quite as cool as being Mrs. Bloom, but still pretty cool. She was liking the idea, too.

"Yeah, we could put in a bunch of stuff about us, and then in twenty years, PCA students could dig it up and see what we were like." Zoey looked at her friends to see what they thought. This could be a really cool project!

"I think that's an excellent idea. Let's make it a class project." Mr. Bender was totally on board.

"So what do we have to do?" Lola asked.

"Everyone should pick an item that best represents who you are right now," Mr. Bender instructed.

"And then we put it all in a container and bury it somewhere on campus?" Zoey asked.

"That's the idea." Bender nodded, smiling.

Chase absently flipped another page in the eighties yearbook. His eyes bugged out. "Whoa, Mr. Bender — you used to be a *cheerleader*?" he asked, trying to hide the laughter in his voice.

A crowd of kids pushed closer to see Bender with pom-poms. The curly-haired teacher rushed forward and snapped up the yearbook. "There were no girls here!" he defended himself. The kids kept laughing as Mr. Bender took his yearbook and what was left of his pride to his desk at the front of the room.

CHAPTER 10

Give It a Rest

"Yeah. Oooh, that's hot. Yeah, you're lookin' good." Logan tapped the arrow keys on his laptop, scrolling through photos of his favorite subject — himself. His image appeared both on the screen of his laptop and on his giant TV. "Whassup, handsome?" he crooned as yet another enormous picture of himself, wearing a cap and tank top, filled the huge flat-screen monitor.

From the couch behind Logan, Chase and Michael tried to ignore their self-absorbed friend as they went through CDs, looking for inspiration. But Logan and his twenty-zillion head shots were hard to ignore.

"Okay, there's a fifty-fifty chance I am gonna puke," Chase confided as he glanced at the Logan-filled screen. Logan wasn't a bad-looking guy, but his egomania was enough to make any normal guy queasy.

Michael shot Chase a look and edged toward the

other side of the sofa. He didn't want to be anywhere near his roommate if he lost his lunch. "I'm gonna sit over here, then."

"What are you doing, anyway?" Chase asked, looking over at Logan. He was well aware of Logan's extra-large ego, but the photo montage deserved a little explanation.

"Trying to decide which picture of myself to put in the time capsule." Logan scrolled to the next picture of himself. It was a shot of him looking straight into the camera with his arms over his head. A keeper. "Niiiice," Logan remarked, pumping his fist in the air.

Well, maybe for him. "Okay, that's *enough*." Michael grabbed the remote for the flat screen and flicked it off. "I do *not* need to look at your armpit shrubs."

"*Thank you*," Chase said gratefully as the screen went black. Sometimes Logan was practically impossible to take.

"So what are *you* guys putting in the time capsule?" Logan asked, grabbing a soda from the mini fridge.

"Well, ya know, we're writing a song about our lives here at PCA," Chase answered, eyeing the stack of CDs on his lap.

"I'm doing the music," Michael said, twirling a drumstick and nodding.

"I'm writing the lyrics," Chase added. He was really excited about their idea, but writing lyrics was turning out to be harder than he'd thought. And so far the CDs he'd looked at weren't helping.

"Oh, so it goes like, 'I love you, Zoey, from my head down to my toey'?" Logan cracked himself up in a lovesick imitation of Chase.

"No," Chase replied, laughing to hide his embarrassment.

Logan shook his head and waved the guys off before leaving the room.

As soon as Logan was out the door, Chase grabbed a pen and started writing. He might be able to use that. . . .

"Don't write that down!" Michael shot Chase a horrified look and Chase set down the pad and pen as quickly as he had picked them up.

"You were going to write that down, weren't you?" Michael prodded. He couldn't believe it. He wanted their song to be good, not dorky!

"Maybe," Chase admitted with a sheepish nod.

"Hey, Zo', you coming to bed?" Nicole asked. They were in their dorm lounge and it was kind of late. Nicole was already in her jammies and on her way to their room with a load of clean laundry.

Zoey was busy fiddling with power cords. Her laptop was connected to a camcorder on a tripod. "Nah," Zoey answered. "I'm working on my time capsule thing." She made some adjustments and pushed a button on the camera.

"'Kay, have fun," Nicole said with a smile as she headed out with her pile of clothes.

"'Night," Zoey called. When Nicole was gone, Zoey was alone in the lounge. Perfect. She wouldn't have any more interruptions. Settling herself on the couch opposite the camera, Zoey aimed a remote and pushed the record button. The red light appeared and Zoey was on.

"Hi. I'm Zoey Brooks," Zoey introduced herself to the camera. She tried to imagine the people who would receive her message. "If you're watching this, it must be twenty years from now. I bet a lot of stuff's changed since I went to PCA." Zoey paused, squinting at her computer camera setup. Her laptop was working like a monitor, so she could actually see herself and what she was burning onto a DVD as she did it — it was all pretty techie and cool.

"Hmm," Zoey said thoughtfully. Technology was

constantly changing. Could that be an issue in twenty years? "I hope you guys still have DVD players in the future, 'cause if not, I'm talking to no one," she joked. "Anyway, for me, the *best* part of PCA is spending time with my friends. And I'm lucky 'cause I have *awesome* friends here. . . ." Zoey trailed off. She thought she was alone in the lounge, but on the monitor she spotted an elderly man lingering behind her with his broom, waving at the camera.

Zoey turned around slowly. "Hello," she said, feeling a little weirded out. What did he want?

"What are you doing, making a tape?" he asked in a gravelly voice.

"Uh-huh," Zoey answered. Wasn't it obvious?

"For what?" he asked.

"A class."

"What's it about?" The old guy was full of questions.

"Ummmm . . . I'm talking about my friends and stuff," she replied, trying not to sound rude. Why did he need to know?

"You want me to be in it?" the janitor offered. He straightened the collar on his jumpsuit and smoothed his thinning gray hair in case he had a close-up.

"No . . . not really," Zoey answered. What she wanted was for him to leave so she could get back to her project.

"Yeah, well, I'm busy," he said grouchily, turning away and sweeping his way toward the door.

Zoey picked up the remote and hit stop. "Okaaay, we don't wanna scare the people of the future, so let's start this again," she said to herself, feeling a tiny bit guilty. She was sure the janitor wasn't trying to be creepy, but . . .

"Hi. I'm Zoey Brooks. . . ." Zoey started again.

In her room with Lola, Nicole surveyed a giant pile of clothes on her bed. She picked up a pink terry spaghetti strap dress, looked it over, and tossed it back onto the pile. Then she retrieved a flowery pink dress with satin trim. "Okay, what do you think of this dress? Do you like this dress?" Nicole held it up for Lola to see.

Lola barely looked up from the magazine she was reading. "It's good for *you*," she answered, sounding totally bored. Nicole had been showing her clothes for what felt like hours. Couldn't the girl just make up her mind? It was late, and she wanted to go to sleep!

"Yeah," Nicole said, still contemplating the dress, "but it's, like, so two months ago. How about this top? You like this top?" She held a sleeveless red-and-white floral shirt up in front of the PCA T-shirt she slept in. The red shirt was one of her favorites. "It makes me look chesty," she confided to Lola in a whisper.

"Okay, can you explain to me why you wanna put your *clothes* in the time capsule?" Lola asked. She preferred to keep her clothes in the closet where she could, like, wear them.

"'Cause, I think the PCA students of the future will be very interested to know how cutely I dressed," Nicole burbled. Duh.

"You are so deep," Lola said with a straight face.

Her sarcasm was lost on Nicole. "Thanks." Nicole beamed, tossing the shirt back onto her bed.

"So what are *you* putting in the time capsule?" Nicole asked. Lola hadn't said anything about what she was going to do.

"Nothing," Lola said casually, turning back to her mag.

Nicole's eyes went wide. "How come?" she asked. The time capsule was going to be so cool, she couldn't imagine not wanting to contribute something.

"'Cause twenty years from now I'll be an extremely famous movie star, so if anyone wants to know about me they can watch my *True Hollywood Story*," Lola explained matter-of-factly.

"Okay, but if you don't turn in something, you're gonna get a zero," Nicole reminded her.

"Don't worry. I'll get credit." Lola did not sound at all worried about her grade.

"But —"

Before Nicole could worry about it anymore, Lola reached up and turned out the light. Enough was enough.

"And now it's dark," Nicole said, still standing by the bunk and wondering what to do next.

"So go to bed," Lola suggested.

"Fine," Nicole said with a sigh. She climbed her ladder, shoved the clothes aside, and got under her covers.

For a brief moment the room was silent. Then a sound like an angry hibernating bear filled the room. Lola and Nicole both groaned. Quinn was snoring . . . again!

Lola snapped on the lights. She'd had it. "Are we supposed to put up with that snoring every night?" she asked. She was sick of having her beauty sleep interrupted. An actress had to look her best. "Someone's gotta say something," Lola fumed.

"And what are we gonna say to her?" Nicole asked. "'Quinn, you gotta quit snoring'? We can't say that."

Why not? Lola jumped out of bed, crossed the room, and pounded on Quinn's wall with her palm. "Quinn! You gotta quit snoring!" she yelled. She kept pounding until the snoring stopped. She glanced at Nicole and shrugged. It was worth it. And half a second later all was quiet. They did it!

But before they could celebrate, or get to sleep, Quinn's face appeared on the monitor she'd installed in their room. She looked annoyed. "Hey," she said into the camera, "will you guys quit banging on the wall? I'm trying to sleep."

CHAPTER 11

Talking About You

Zoey popped a grape into her mouth as she walked up a wide flight of stairs with Chase. He was telling her about the song he and Michael were working on for the time capsule. Lately, all anyone could talk about was the time capsule and what they were putting inside it. And from the sound of it, there were going to be all kinds of different stuff included.

"... So I think it'll be pretty cool. Michael laid down this awesome keyboard track, and I should finish the lyrics by tomorrow night."

Zoey nodded, impressed. A song was a great idea. "So do I get to hear the song before you guys put it in the time capsule?" she asked, flicking her side ponytail over her shoulder.

"I dunno," Chase teased. "What's it worth to ya?"

"Mmmm." Zoey contemplated her snack, breaking

off a small cluster of fruit. "'Bout fifteen grapes?" she offered.

"Deal." Chase grinned and accepted the grapes. "So what about you? You finish making your time capsule DVD?"

"Yep. Last night," Zoey answered. She had stayed up late doing it — thanks to the janitorial interruption — and had to rush this morning to get ready. Not that anyone could tell. She looked totally pulled together in her cap-sleeve top and plaid skirt.

"Yeah? So what'd you talk about?" Chase asked. This could be interesting.

"Y'know, all about my life here at PCA . . . my thoughts, my friends, what I like to do for fun . . ." Zoey had ended up saying a lot, actually. Making the DVD was more involved than she'd thought it would be.

"Your friends?" Chase was curious. What he really wanted to know was if she had said anything about him. But he didn't want to pry.

"Uh-huh." Zoey nodded.

"Oh. So . . . like, you talked about Nicole and Lola . . . and Quinn. . . ." Chase was fishing. He couldn't help himself.

"Yeah. And you and Michael. Even Logan a little

72

bit," Zoey admitted, rolling her eyes. She had been surprised to find herself talking about Logan.

"Really? So, what kind of stuff did you say about . . .
everybody?" Chase tried to sound casual even though
he was dying to know more.

"Y'know . . . different stuff for different people,"
Zoey said vaguely. She wasn't sure what Chase was getting at. She just talked a little about everybody.

"'Course. That makes sense. 'Cause, like, if you're
talking about Logan, you might mention that he's an
egomaniac. . . ." Chase said, trying to draw out more
information.

"Right . . ." Zoey was starting to see where Chase
was going with this. He wanted to know what she'd said
about him!

". . . But if you were talkin' about . . . *me*, you might
say . . . what?" There. It was out.

Zoey smiled playfully. She knew what Chase wanted
to know, but she'd made her DVD for the eyes and ears of
the future. "I'm not telling you what I said," she told him.

"Oh, I think you are," Chase replied. Maybe she'd
go for it.

"*Sorreee*," Zoey said in singsong. "Gotta get to
class." She loved keeping him in suspense.

"Oh, c'mon. What'd you say about me?" Chase called after Zoey's retreating back.

"You'll find out in twenty years," Zoey called over her shoulder. She gave Chase a small wave.

Frozen in place, Chase watched her go. Not only did he have no idea what Zoey had said in her time capsule entry, he did not know what he was going to say in his, either.

Michael's voice echoed in his head. "All right, I added the drum track last night and did a rough mix. How are you coming with the lyrics?"

Good question. A question without an answer.

That night in their room Michael asked again. "Yo, *Chase!*" he yelled, trying to snap Chase out of whatever trance he was in. He was waiting for an answer.

"*What?*" Chase yelled. "I mean, yes?" he guessed at the answer Michael was looking for.

"You don't even know what I asked you," Michael said accusingly.

Chase sighed loudly, put down his pencil and pad, and stood up. "I'm sorry, man. I can't focus." He started to pace. "All I can think about is what Zoey might have said about me on her DVD."

Michael lifted his eyes to the heavens. "Kill me," he pleaded.

"I mean, does she like me as a friend? More than a friend? How does she feel about hats?"

Hold on. Michael was suddenly confused. "You don't wear hats," he pointed out.

"I know, but if she *likes* hats, I could give 'em a try. I just need to know her *feelings*." Chase held out his open hands.

Michael shook his head. This was worse than he thought. It was time for some *real* advice. "Okay. You wanna know how Zoey feels about you? Ask her."

"No! I just wanna find out what she said about me on her DVD!" Chase blurted as Logan walked into the room.

"Zoey talked about you on her DVD?" Logan asked. His backpack was slung over his shoulder. He was wearing a black sleeveless T-shirt and looked, as always, laid-back.

"Um, yeah." Chase had not been expecting his other roommate back for a while. "But I don't care," he said, trying to play it cool but knowing it wouldn't work.

"Sure you don't." Logan chuckled. He knew better. Way better.

"I don't," Chase insisted, shaking his dark curls.

"Fine," Logan said smoothly. "Just remember:

Tomorrow that DVD gets buried ... deep down in the ground ... for the next *twenty years.*" He put special emphasis on the last two words. He knew it would drive Chase nuts. And driving Chase nuts was one of his favorite pastimes.

CHAPTER 12

Sleep Deprived

Nicole yawned as she stumbled into the Brenner Hall lounge in a brightly colored striped tank top, shorts, and slippers. She glanced around, looking for the spot where the noise was coming from. The snoring noise. She spotted Quinn almost immediately and blinked in surprise. You never knew what to expect from Quinn, but this was even stranger than usual.

The resident brain was dressed in her jammies, hanging upside down by her feet from some crazy contraption, and snoring . . . loudly. The ends of her long dark ponytails practically touched the floor.

"Quinn? Quinn. Quinn!" Nicole had to shout to wake the girl up.

Quinn's eyes fluttered open. "Oh. Hello. What are you doing here?" she asked casually, as if hanging upside down in the girls' lounge was what everyone did.

"I got up to use the bathroom. Then I heard your *insane* snoring," Nicole said, crossing her arms over her chest. The snoring was really getting out of control. She hadn't slept through an entire night in days.

"I'm still snoring?" Quinn asked, sounding disappointed and surprised all at once.

"Louder than ever," Nicole confirmed.

"Darn it. I thought that sleeping upside down would invert my nasal cavities and stop me from snoring. And this is the third thing I've tried." Quinn sounded really upset, like she was about to cry.

"Wow, I thought you could figure out anything." Nicole was stunned. Quinn's solutions were always unconventional, and not always necessary, but they usually worked — even if it wasn't exactly how she planned. She was, hands down, the smartest student at PCA.

"I can, usually. But I can't monitor my own snoring 'cause I'm asleep when it happens," Quinn lamented. She was truly puzzled by this problem and was starting to feel hopeless.

Nicole stifled another yawn. She wished she was asleep when Quinn's snoring happened, too. She wished she was asleep right now. "Yeah, well —" Nicole pointed toward the exit and struggled to come up with a reason to go.

"Hey!" Quinn interrupted. She obviously had an idea. "Will you help me?"

Nicole would do anything to stop Quinn's snoring. But she had seen the totally strange stuff that happened to people who assisted Quinn with her experiments. "Um, I don't think I'm the right person to —"

"Please?" Quinn begged. "I just need you to monitor my snoring while I try a few other remedies."

"Well . . ." Nicole gave in, not really having a choice. Besides, maybe it would help Quinn stop snoring. "Sure. I guess I can do that."

"Yay!" Quinn clapped her hands gleefully. She was back on track. "Okay, you can start by helping me get down from here."

"Right." Nicole reached for the biggest, most obvious lever on the crazy machine. It had to be the release.

"Wait, don't pull that lev —" Quinn shouted, but too late. The lever released her feet and she dropped to the floor like a rock. Ouch.

Nicole cringed and looked down at the pile of Quinn on the floor. Her leg was over her head in a totally unnatural position. And she was making strange strangling noises. "Careful," Nicole cried, wincing. Quinn looked *totally* uncomfortable.

CHAPTER 13

Deep Underground

"You didn't bring *anything* to put in the time capsule?" Zoey asked Lola. She couldn't believe it. Lola seemed to like herself a lot — too much, almost. Why wouldn't she want to put something about herself in the capsule?

The more she learned about her new roommate, the less she felt she really knew her. Today was the day they were loading the capsule, and Lola had arrived on the grassy field empty-handed — after telling Mr. Bender what a cool idea she thought it was.

"Don't worry about it." Lola shook her head. Her large hoop earrings swung around her face.

"He's gonna give you a zero," Zoey cautioned. Mr. Bender was nice, but not that nice.

"We'll see." Lola shrugged, touching her pink crocheted hat that went with her dramatic Bohemian look.

She had funky green streaks in her long straight hair, and wore a chunky beaded choker and a racer-back tank over a long-sleeve pink top.

Zoey shrugged and turned to watch the capsule being loaded. Mr. Bender was checking kids off his list as they added their contributions.

Nicole dropped in her best threads — silently bidding the outfit good-bye. She would miss it! Behind her, Logan walked up to the capsule carrying his contribution. Nicole blinked. Was that really a picture of himself?

"You're putting in a picture of yourself?" Nicole asked incredulously. Everyone knew Logan had a giant ego, but still!

"That's right," Logan replied easily, uncapping a pen. Not only was he putting his precious photo in, he was autographing it. "Dear hot girls of the future... you're welcome," he said aloud as he wrote the words. Nicole rolled her eyes as Logan carefully placed his framed photo in the capsule. Then, kissing the pen, he tossed it in after — a little bonus for the girls of the future.

"Anywhere in here?" Zoey asked, stepping up to the capsule, holding her DVD.

"Yep," Mr. Bender said. "Just toss 'er in."

Zoey added her DVD to the collection and walked away feeling satisfied. She hoped the students twenty years from now liked it.

"Chase, Michael, what do you guys have?" Mr. Bender asked as the guys approached.

"We wrote a song about our life here at PCA," Michael explained.

"Cool." Mr. Bender smiled his approval and Chase tossed the CD in. He could see Zoey's DVD sitting on top of the pile and had to use all of his restraint to keep himself from grabbing it and running away. Finally he turned away, giving Mr. Bender a little salute.

Lola approached the time capsule next.

"Lola, what'd you bring?" Mr. Bender asked.

Without any warning Lola burst into tears.

"What? What's the matter?" Mr. Bender stepped forward to comfort the stricken student.

"You're just gonna have to give me a zero for this project," Lola sobbed dramatically.

"You didn't pick an item?" Mr. Bender asked gently.

"No, I did," Lola explained between sobs. "It was a locket that my grandmother gave me — before she ... left us."

"Aww. I'm so sorry." Mr. Bender shook his head.

"My dad tells me I'm just like her," Lola went on,

struggling through her tears, "so I thought the locket would be perfect for the time capsule, but . . ."

"But what?" Mr. Bender asked gently.

Lola clutched her chest where the locket would hang. "I . . . I just can't. It's all I have left of her. I'm sorry!"

Fighting back tears, Lola looked at her teacher. He was choked up. "It's okay," Mr. Bender consoled her. "Look, you gave the assignment a lot of thought, and that's the important thing."

"Really?" Lola gasped.

"'Course. And don't worry — I'm gonna give you full credit," Mr. Bender assured her.

"Thank you so much." Lola's crying stopped as quickly as it had started. She wiped her eyes. Then, turning quickly, she grinned at Zoey and Nicole. "Acting!" she said quietly as she passed them. Her two roommates watched in disbelief as she walked away.

"Okay," Mr. Bender said, pulling himself together after Lola's sob story. "I think that's everything. Let's bury this puppy!"

With the help of two older boys, the capsule was lowered into a hole.

Chase watched, downcast, as his dreams of finding out Zoey's true feelings were buried.

"Guess you won't know what Zoey thinks of you for another *twenty years*." Logan couldn't stop himself from rubbing it in, just a little. Torturing Chase about Zoey was way too easy.

Chase stared at the sealed and disappearing-under-the-dirt time capsule sadly. Without a word he bid his hopes *adieu*.

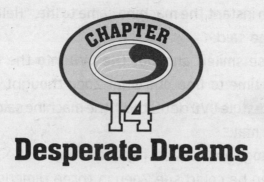

CHAPTER 14

Desperate Dreams

Chase rolled over in his bed fitfully. Outside, lightning flashed. Rain drummed on the dorm roof.

"Guess you won't know what Zoey thinks of you for another *twenty years*," Logan's voice taunted for the hundredth time.

Finally Chase drifted off to sleep. He dreamed that he was in the future . . . twenty years in the future, to be exact. He still had a mop of curly dark hair, but his casual shorts, tees, and plaid button-downs had given way to a space-age metallic silver suit. He held Zoey's DVD in his hand.

"Finally!" dream-Chase exclaimed. "I get to watch it!"

He walked up to his audio/video machine. It looked totally high-tech, yet had no buttons. "Player on," he said simply.

In an instant the machine came to life. "Hello, Chase," the machine said.

Chase smiled and put the DVD into the player. At last it was time to find out what Zoey thought of him!

"Old-style DVD detected," the machine said. "Choose display format."

"Hologram," Chase replied. Why settle for a flat image when he could see Zoey in three dimensions? In a minute Zoey would be standing right in front of him!

"Thank you," the machine said. "Image playback."

Chase walked over to a molded plastic chair and sat down. His heart was thudding in his chest, and his palms were sweaty. The time of truth had come.

Suddenly a bright light shot down from a cylinder on the ceiling. Then Zoey appeared.

"There are so many things I can say about Chase," she began. "For one thing, he's the first person I met at PCA. And we've gotten to be really close friends. But there is something I've never told Chase, and that is . . ."

"Chase . . . Chase!" a voice interrupted.

Zoey's hologram image began to flicker.

"That is *what*?" Chase asked desperately as Zoey's image faded in and out.

"Chase . . ." came the interrupting voice again.

"And that is . . ." Zoey's sketchy hologram repeated.

Chase felt panicked. "C'mon, finish the sentence! Zoey! Zoey, come back!" he cried.

"Chase!" The interrupting voice just wouldn't quit. It was Michael, who was trying to jostle his roommate awake.

"Say it!" Chase screamed. "Zoey, come back!"

"Chase!" Michael called, giving his roomie a good shake. The dude was losing it!

Chase opened his eyes wide and bolted upright, cracking his head on the bunk bed above him. "Ow!" he shouted. He threw off his covers and leaped to his feet. "Michael!" he shouted, grabbing his roommate by the shoulders. "You wrecked my dream! I was just about to hear what Zoey said about me on her DVD!" He looked desperate. "Man, why'd you wake me up?"

Michael felt totally guilty. "I wanted to know if you have an extra pillow I could borrow," he said, suddenly really regretting his decision to wake Chase up. He was totally freaked out about this Zoey thing. And now Michael was going to have to hear all about it. . . .

Chase snatched a pillow off his bed and threw it at Michael, hitting him in the head. "Here!" he shouted. "Now lemme get back to my dream!"

Chase dove back onto his bed and pulled the covers over him. He closed his eyes tightly. Michael just stared at him. And then, ten seconds later . . .

"Am I asleep?" Chase asked miserably.

"No." Michael shook his head.

Chase jumped back onto his feet and grabbed some tools. They had a mission to see to. "Come with me!" he ordered.

"Where?" Michael asked, not really wanting to know the answer. It was the middle of the night, and Chase's ideas were crazy in the middle of the *day*.

"We gotta dig up that time capsule," Chase said.

Michael stared at Chase. He had definitely lost it. "Dude, it's two o'clock in the morning!"

"I've gotta know what Zoey said about me!" Chase begged. "I need your help!"

Michael could feel himself getting sucked in. But he wasn't going down without a fight. "Are you insane?" he asked pointedly.

Half an hour later Chase and Michael were out in the pouring rain with two shovels and a ton of mud. They dug and dug and dug. Rain lashed at their clothes. Mud splattered all over their faces and arms. They were soaking wet. And still they dug. . . .

"You're insane!" Michael insisted, knowing that

he was crazy, too. He didn't care about Zoey's DVD. So what was he doing out here in a thunderstorm, covered in mud?

"Just keep digging!" Chase ordered.

"What do you think I'm doin'," Michael shot back, "having a shrimp cocktail? Man, I tell ya, of all the crazy —"

At last Chase's shovel hit something hard. "Ahhh! Here it is!" he yelled over the rain. "C'mon, help me lift it outta here!"

Chase and Michael tossed their shovels aside and began to paw at the wet dirt with their hands.

"Help me!" Chase shrieked, flinging mud off the capsule. He was so close he could taste it!

"I'm trying," Michael panted. The dirt around the time capsule was so wet it was oozing back around the metal tube as quickly as they cleared it. Finally they found the ends and pulled it out of the sucking mud.

Chase yanked open the time capsule door and pawed at the contents inside. At last he found Zoey's DVD. Raising it into the air, he looked up at the dark sky and cackled. "Finally, it's mine! It's all mine!" He sounded a little like a crazy scientist who had successfully completed an experiment. And he looked . . . well . . .

Michael stared at his friend, wide-eyed. Plastered

with rain and mud, Chase looked freaky and sounded even freakier. There was *noooo* question — Chase had definitely lost it.

Chase laughed again, then stopped abruptly when he caught Michael's eye. Michael was giving him the "you've gone around the bend" look. "I found the DVD," Chase explained sheepishly.

"Really?" Michael replied, as if he'd had no idea. As if he had not been helping him the entire time.

Chase felt kind of like a dork, but he didn't care. In just a few minutes he'd know what Zoey Brooks thought of him. But first he had to cover his tracks. . . .

"C'mon," he said to his partner in crime. "Help me rebury the time capsule so know one knows we dug it up."

Michael rolled his eyes. "Sure," he said. Why not? "What else do I have to do at three o'clock in the morning?" He grabbed his shovel and started scooping the mud back on top of the time capsule. What a night.

CHAPTER 15
Go Fish

It was three o'clock in the morning. Nicole was exhausted. She stared at Quinn sitting across from her on the couch in the girls' lounge. The other girl seemed wide-awake. But if Nicole didn't get to sleep soon, she would be a wreck! Not to mention the fact that she hated it when she got circles under her eyes.

"Quinn, let's just face it. Nothing's ever gonna stop your freakish snoring," she insisted.

Quinn looked determined. A scientist who gave up easily got nowhere! Besides, she had an ace up her sleeve. "Don't give up yet," she told Nicole.

"We've tried everything," Nicole protested. At least, it seemed like they had.

"No." Quinn had a devilish look in her eyes. "We haven't tried these. . . ." She held up a glass of water and gazed lovingly at her "ace," or aces, since there were two of them, swimming around inside.

Nicole peered into the glass and made a face. "Ewww!" she cried, jumping back. "What are those?"

"A very rare breed of guppy from South Africa," Quinn said proudly.

Nicole shot Quinn a look. "Okay, and how are South African guppies gonna stop you from snoring?" she asked, not sure she wanted to hear the answer. It could be anything with Quinn.

"Well," Quinn explained, "when you remove them from the water, they secrete a sticky liquid that's supposed to numb the mucus membranes of humans."

"And?" Nicole was totally confused. What was she talking about? She couldn't possibly be saying that she was going to . . .

"If I stick these up my nose, they'll coat my inner nostrils and the numbing effect should stop my snoring," Quinn said casually, as if she were talking about the weather.

Nicole stared at Quinn. This was a new level of scientific weirdness. A gross level. "Uh, I'm going away now," she said, starting to get up off the couch. She couldn't get away fast enough.

Quinn pushed Nicole back onto one of the cushions.

"I need you to stay here so you can watch me sleep and tell me if it works. Ready?" She reached into the glass and grabbed a guppy. Nicole envisioned one of the guppies flopping out of Quinn's nostril and landing on her arm. Or leg. Or face! "Noooo," she said, feeling panicked.

Quinn held the first guppy up to her nose and inhaled deeply. The slimy little creature slid right into her nasal cavity. It felt . . . invigorating! She scooped up the second guppy and sniffed again. Slip! Very satisfying. And now the experiment could begin.

Nicole stared at Quinn in disgust. The guppies had completely disappeared into her nose. They were in her body! Quinn had snorted live fish into her nose. It was even grosser than Lola drinking raw eggs! "This is the most disturbing moment of my life," she moaned.

Moment of Truth

Chase sat alone on the bottom bunk. Above him, Michael slept soundly in his muddy clothes. Across the room, Logan was out like a hibernating bear. A pair of filthy shovels leaned against the wall.

Chase opened his computer and the glow from the screen softly lit the room. He opened the jewel case and pulled out Zoey's DVD. Hands shaking slightly, he slipped it into the machine and put on his headphones. Then he clicked the menu to play the DVD.

In an instant Zoey's pretty face appeared on his screen. Chase smiled. Zoey was the greatest.

"Uh . . . hi. I'm Zoey Brooks and if you're watching this it must be twenty years from now. I bet a lot of stuff's changed since —"

Chase clicked the scan-forward button anxiously. He needed to get to the part about him before he lost his nerve. Now that he had the DVD and could find out the truth, he was feeling a little . . . guilty.

He clicked once more and Zoey's face came back into focus. Her voice was like music to Chase's ears. ". . . so having Nicole as my roommate is definitely one of the best things about my life here at PCA. And now, I wanna tell you about one of the most special people I've ever met. His name is Chase Matthews and he's like the most —"

Click. Pause. Chase's heart thudded in his chest. This was it — what he'd been so desperate to find out! And no one was going to stop him from listening to the rest of the DVD. Nobody except himself.

Chase stared at Zoey's paused face. Even now she looked beautiful. So why did he feel so bad?

Setting the computer aside, Chase got out of bed and nudged Michael. "Michael . . . dude, wake up! Michael . . ." He needed his friend to wake up so he could talk to him.

Michael rolled over with a groan. "Michael's asleep," he replied groggily. "Leave a message at the beep. *Beep.*" He rolled over again, this time putting his back to Chase.

Chase reached up and rolled him back over. "C'mon. I gotta talk to you," Chase pleaded.

Michael opened his eyes groggily. Hadn't Chase

messed with his sleep enough for one night? "Aw, what now, man? You want me to go scuba diving?" he quipped.

"Is this wrong?" Chase asked, getting right to the point.

Waking up a friend who was trying to sleep after you'd forced him to do your bidding in the middle of the night? Michael thought. It sure felt wrong. But he was pretty sure that wasn't what Chase was talking about. "Is what wrong?" he asked.

Chase sighed heavily. "For me to watch Zoey's DVD without her permission. Is it wrong?"

Michael looked at Chase. The dude had a problem. "Does it feel wrong?" he asked.

Chase was quiet for a second. He didn't want it to, but he had to admit it did. "Kinda," he said.

Michael nodded. "Then you don't need to ask me what you already know." He pulled the covers up and rolled over yet again, hoping that Chase was finished with him for at *least* two or three hours.

Chase sat down on his bed. He picked up his laptop. He could still see Zoey's squiggly, freeze-framed face. With a giant sigh, he ejected the DVD and snapped it back into its case. After closing his computer he got to his feet, shoved the DVD into his pocket, grabbed a shovel, and headed back out into the rain, alone.

CHAPTER 17

Amphibian Fix

Sun poured through the windows of the girls' lounge. While female students made their way through the common room on their way to breakfast and class, Quinn and Nicole snoozed peacefully on the couch. There wasn't a snore to be heard.

Zoey opened the door to the lounge and looked around. She hadn't seen Nicole since the day before and had no idea where she was. But it only took a couple of seconds to spot her on the couch with Quinn. Both of them were totally zonked out.

Lola walked over and nudged the sleeping pair with her knee. "Hey, guys," she said gruffly. And then, "*hey!*" really loudly. She wasn't used to being ignored.

Zoey nudged Nicole more gently. "Nicole, it's morning," she said.

Nicole stirred awake and rolled off the couch. She

looked around sleepily. "Oh, hey, guys," she greeted her roommates with a yawn. "I guess we overslept." She blinked again as her own words sank in. "We over*slept!*" she cried jubilantly. "Quinn! Wake up! Get up!" She was so excited she couldn't sit still.

"What?" Quinn asked groggily, sitting up and adjusting her glasses.

"We slept through the night!" Nicole exclaimed. Normally she wouldn't call from three in the morning until eight in the morning "through the night," but given it was the most sleep she'd had in a long while, she was feeling generous. *Very* generous.

Quinn looked befuddled. "I didn't snore?" she asked eagerly.

"No! The guppies worked!" Who cared if Quinn had had miniature amphibians up her nose for five hours? She finally got some sleep!

"The guppies worked!" Quinn echoed, feeling tingly all over. Nothing felt better than a successful experiment.

Lola wrinkled her nose in confusion. "Did she say guppies?" she asked.

Zoey nodded warily. With Quinn, anything was possible. "I heard guppies," she confirmed.

"South African guppies," Nicole said with empha- sis. "She put 'em up her nose," she added casually.

"Yeah!" Quinn agreed. "See?"

She picked up her glass of water, closed one nos- tril with a finger, and blew hard. *Plop!* One of the guppies fell right into the water. She did it again with the other nostril. *Splash!* The little guys swam around happily. Quinn held up the glass. "Look!"

Zoey leaned forward and peered into the glass. It looked surprisingly . . . clean. "Yeah, those are guppies," she agreed.

Lola nodded, her brown eyes wide. And she thought her goth act was weird.

Just then Coco, their dorm adviser, walked through the lounge, carrying a jar of peanut butter and laughing to herself. "Hey, girls," she greeted, pausing next to Zoey. "You guys catch Leno last night?" she asked.

"No."

"Nope."

"Uh-uh."

"Oh, you missed a gem. He did this joke about how slow the mail is . . . it killed me . . . he goes . . ."

Suddenly Coco started to cough.

". . . he says, 'The mail is so slow . . .'"

She coughed again, a lot harder. She definitely had a glob of peanut butter in her throat.

"Are you all right?" Zoey asked, starting to worry a little. She almost looked like she was choking.

Coco coughed, then made a little gagging sound. Unable to talk, she grabbed the glass of water out of Quinn's hand.

"Wait!"

"No!"

"Don't drink th —!"

Coco ignored them and gulped the water — and the guppies — down. "Oh, that's better," she announced, waving a hand in front of her face. "Wooo."

Zoey, Lola, Nicole, and Quinn all stared, unable to talk. It was just too gross for words.

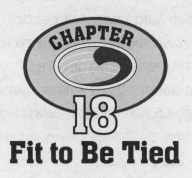

CHAPTER 18

Fit to Be Tied

It was another gorgeous afternoon on the PCA campus. Kids were all over the place laughing, hanging out, and heading to class. Zoey was riding along on her Jet-X scooter enjoying the feel of the wind in her hair. Now that Quinn had stopped snoring and that Lola was acting more or less normal, life at PCA was great again.

Zoey steered along the path, careful not to crash into anyone. Out of the corner of her eye she spotted something . . . interesting. Chase was lying facedown on the grass, fast asleep. Zoey smiled to herself, parked her scooter, and walked over to him. He was out like a light.

Walking around to his feet, she carefully tied his shoelaces together. Then she went back to the other end of him and lay down so they were head to head.

Zoey cleared her throat, and Chase's head bobbed up. They were almost nose to nose on the grass.

"Hey," Zoey said cheerfully.

"Hello," Chase replied. Waking up to Zoey's smiling face was a treat he wasn't expecting.

"Whatcha doin'?" Zoey asked, her eyes sparkling.

"Resting," Chase said. It was kind of obvious, wasn't it?

"Why?" Zoey wanted to know. Was Logan's stereo back in action? Was someone in Chase's dorm snoring, too?

"'Cause I haven't gotten much sleep in the past couple of days," Chase admitted.

"How come?" Zoey pressed.

Chase was starting to feel a little nervous. Did Zoey know what he'd been up to? Should he confess? "Just busy . . . doin' stuff," he offered, choosing to play dumb instead.

Zoey nodded and tried not to smirk. Chase had no idea there was a practical joke in the works. She knew she shouldn't tease her friend but couldn't help it. Chase was so gullible. "Yeah, stuff can keep you busy."

"Yeah," Chase agreed.

"So listen . . ." Zoey sounded thoughtful, like she was about to spill something important.

"Okay," Chase said, a little excited. He picked up

on the tone in Zoey's voice. She was going to tell him something . . . something big.

"You know how you asked me what I said about you on my DVD?"

"Uh-huh." Chase could hardly believe his ears.

"And I said you'll find out in twenty years?"

"Right," Chase said slowly.

"I decided that was a little mean," Zoey admitted.

"You did?" Chase struggled not to lose his cool.

"Mmm-hmm."

"Sooo?" Chase prodded. The suspense was killing him!

"So I'm gonna tell ya," Zoey said.

"You're gonna *tell me*?" Chase echoed. He couldn't believe it.

"Yep," Zoey promised with a smile, then dropped the bomb. "In ten years," she added, getting to her feet.

"What?!" Chase cried, totally exasperated. That was still mean.

"*Ciao!*" Zoey called with a little giggle as she ran over to her Jet-X.

"Oh, you're dead," Chase threatened with a laugh. Zoey sure knew how to harass a guy.

"Ooooh, I'm scaaared!" Zoey held up her hands in mock fear.

Chase scrambled to his feet to go after her but tripped almost immediately. He looked down to see his shoelaces tightly tied together. Zoey!

"Okay, now you're really dead!" he called.

Zoey swung a leg over the seat of her Jet-X. "Gotta catch me to kill me!" she called playfully.

Chase scrambled to untie his shoelaces as Zoey started to drive away. As she headed up the path, he yelled after her, "Zoey! I know where you live!" Sure, Chase was a little chapped at the joke Zoey had just played on him, but teasing Zoey and being teased by her were fun and totally normal. And Chase had to admit, he was ready for things to get back to normal. Totally, completely ready.

Want to read more about Zoey
and her friends at PCA?
Then look for these great books!

Girls Got Game
Dramarama
Pranks for Nothing
Beach Party
Spring Break-Up